Smithsonian Prehistoric Zone

Tyrannosaurus Rex

by Gerry Bailey
Illustrated by Karen Carr

Crabtree Publishing Company

www.crabtreebooks.com

Crabtree Publishing Company

www.crabtreebooks.com

Author
Gerry Bailey

Illustrator
Karen Carr

Editorial coordinator
Kathy Middleton

Editor
Lynn Peppas

Proofreader
Kathy Middleton

Prepress technician
Samara Parent

Print and production coordinator
Katherine Berti

Library of Congress Cataloging-in-Publication Data

Bailey, Gerry.
Tyrannosaurus rex / by Gerry Bailey ; illustrated by Karen Carr.
  p. cm. -- (Smithsonian prehistoric zone)
Includes index.
ISBN 978-0-7787-1819-2 (pbk. : alk. paper) -- ISBN 978-0-7787-1806-2 (reinforced library binding : alk. paper) -- ISBN 978-1-4271-9710-8 (electronic (pdf))
1. Tyrannosaurus rex--Juvenile literature. I. Carr, Karen, 1960- ill. II. Title. III. Series.

QE862.S3B36 2011
567.912'9--dc22

2010044035

Library and Archives Canada Cataloguing in Publication

Bailey, Gerry
    Tyrannosaurus rex / by Gerry Bailey ; illustrated
by Karen Carr.

(Smithsonian prehistoric zone)
Includes index.
At head of title: Smithsonian Institution.
Issued also in electronic format.
ISBN 978-0-7787-1806-2 (bound).--ISBN 978-0-7787-1819-2 (pbk.)

    1. Tyrannosaurus rex--Juvenile literature. I. Carr, Karen, 1960- II. Smithsonian Institution III. Title. IV. Series: Bailey, Gerry. Smithsonian prehistoric zone.

QE862.S3B3385 2011   j567.912'9   C2010-906896-3

Crabtree Publishing Company

www.crabtreebooks.com   1-800-387-7650
Copyright © **2011 CRABTREE PUBLISHING COMPANY.**
All rights reserved. No part of this publication may be reproduced, stored in a retrieval system or be transmitted in any form or by any means, electronic, mechanical, photocopying, recording, or otherwise, without the prior written permission of Crabtree Publishing Company. In Canada: we acknowledge the financial support of the Government of Canada through the Canada Book Fund for our publishing activities.

Published in the United States
Crabtree Publishing
PMB 59051
350 Fifth Avenue, 59th Floor
New York, New York 10118

Published in Canada
Crabtree Publishing
616 Welland Ave.
St. Catharines, Ontario
L2M 5V6

Printed in China/012011/GW20101014

Dinosaurs

Living things had been around for billions of years before dinosaurs came along. Animal life on Earth started with single-cell **organisms** that lived in the seas. About 380 million years ago, some animals came out of the sea and onto the land. These were the ancestors that would become the mighty dinosaurs. They were the largest reptiles that have ever lived.

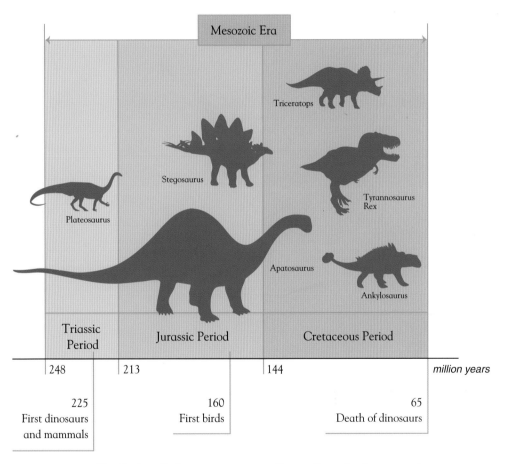

The dinosaur era is called the Mesozoic era. It is divided into three parts called the Triassic, Jurassic, and Cretaceous periods. During the Cretaceous period flowering plants grew for the first time. Plant-eaters, such as *Hadrosaurus*, *Ankylosaurus*, and *Triceratops*, flourished. *Tyrannosaurus rex* may have fed on the herds of plant-eating dinosaurs. Most dinosaurs (except birds) had been wiped out by the end of the Cretaceous period. No is sure exactly why.

Deep in an **ancient** forest, a group of
prehistoric animals drank quietly by a still
pool. There were chattering birds and plant-
eating dinosaurs. It was peaceful and calm.

But lurking out of sight and not far away, there was
danger. It was a giant, terrifying meat-eater called
Tyrannosaurus rex. He was hungry. Suddenly the
animals heard the thud, thud of its huge footsteps.

Tyrannosaurus rex was a frightening **predator**.
It was the biggest meat-eating dinosaur, or
carnivore, to walk the land. It grew up to 39 feet
(12 meters) long and 20 feet (six meters) tall.

It weighed about 7.7 tons (seven metric tons). It was heavier than an African elephant. Inside the gaping jaws of its huge head grew 60 long, sharp teeth.

Tyrannosaurus rex was too slow to catch any of
the animals by the pool. Now he was hungrier
than ever. Then he heard the sound of flapping
wings. It was a flying reptile, or pterodactyl.

Called Quetzalcoatlus, it had long wings made of skin. Tyrannosaurus rex snapped at the creature, but Quetzalcoatlus was too quick. It flew away unharmed. Tyrannosaurus rex grunted angrily.

Perhaps it would be better to look for an animal
to **ambush**. He used his powerful sense of smell
to sniff the air. His huge snout could pick up
smells a long way off. He could smell live **prey**

and dead, rotting animals. He could smell
something across the pool. His keen eyes
picked out movement. There was definitely
something on the other side.

Quickly the great dinosaur plunged into the water and toward the sound. He nearly stepped on a crocodile as his clawed feet splashed through the shallow water.

It had been hiding in the **reeds**. The crocodile had huge jaws of its own, but it was no match for Tyrannosaurus rex.

The movement he had seen was a Triceratops.
It had come to the pool to drink. Tyrannosaurus
was hungry enough to chase after the horned
dinosaur. He had no problem running down his

food as long as the chase was a short one. As he ran, his head and neck were lowered at the front while his tail stuck out at the back for balance. Without his tail, he would fall over.

Tyrannosaurus rex soon caught up with the Triceratops. Up close Triceratops looked dangerous, with its sharp, pointed horns. It would do terrible damage if it struck in the right place.

Those horns could easily pierce an enemy's
stomach or leg. Even Tyrannosaurus rex could
not take a wound like that and survive for long.
He would have to let the Triceratops go.

Tyrannosaurus rex had failed again. He needed to find food in a hurry. He sniffed around once again. This time he picked up a scent coming from a crack in the rocks close by. Slowly he peered in.

A baby Ankylosaurus **cowered** inside. The angry meat-eater tried to force his great jaws into the crack. The Ankylosaurus could feel the Tyrannosaurus's hot breath on its face.

Tyrannosaurus rex snapped again and again,
but could not force his head any further into
the **crevice**. His big head housed a huge skull
and powerful jaw muscles.

Tyrannosaurus rex gave one last mighty lunge.
He bit down on a piece of rock and broke a
tooth. That was enough. He would have to
let this small Ankylosaurus live.

At last Tyrannosaurus rex found a meal.
It was a small Anatotitan. He chased it
with his jaws open and killed it at once.
His terrible teeth did their job.

It had taken a while but at last
Tyrannosaurus rex could eat.
He would not need to hunt
again that day.

Tyrannosaurus rex felt better after his meal.
He wanted to rest. Suddenly a loud, rumbling
noise startled him. It was the sound of a
volcano that was about to **erupt**.

He might be the fiercest predator in the forest but
he was no match for a volcano. Tyrannosaurus
rex hurried away to seek out a safe place.
He would survive to hunt another day.

All about Tyrannosaurus rex

(tye-RAH-nuh-saur-us rex)

Tyrannosaurus rex was one of the largest carnivores, or meat-eating dinosaurs. Its name means "tyrant lizard king."

Tyrannosaurus rex was up to 20 feet (six meters) tall. It grew as tall as a two-storey building. It was 39 feet (12 meters) long, or as long as a school bus. It weighed around 7.7 tons (seven metric tons). Scientists believe that if *Tyrannosaurus* fell down while running,   it would have broken its skull.

Tyrannosaurus rex had huge back legs but very tiny front arms. It also had a second set of ribs on the underside of its body. These might have grown to support its insides when it lay down to rest on its stomach. Its huge jaws were lined with long, sharp teeth that it used to tear flesh and crush bones.

Precambrian Era		570 million years ago			Palaeozoic Era		
Precambrian Period		Cambrian Period	Ordovician Period	Silurian Period	Devonian Period		Carboniferous

380
First life on land

320
First reptiles

The shape of its skull shows that it had a keen sense of smell and very good eyesight. Its sense of smell might have helped it sniff out dead meat. Its keen eyesight makes scientists believe that it was a predator as well as a **scavenger**.

It may have attacked herds of plant-eating dinosaurs, such as *Anatotitan*, by lying in wait for them. Then it would run at them with its powerful jaws open.

Tyrannosaurus bones have been found in western North America and Asia.

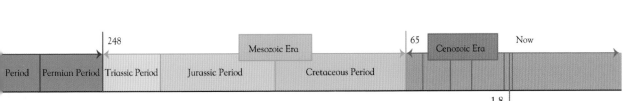

Period	Permian Period	Triassic Period	Jurassic Period	Cretaceous Period			Cenozoic Era	Now
		248		Mesozoic Era		65		
							1.8 First humans	

Big and small

There were several larger dinosaurs but *Tyrannosaurus rex* was one of the big ones. There were small ones too that were no bigger than a chicken. The chart shows the great range in size between the different dinosaurs.

The biggest dinosaurs were gigantic, slow-moving plant-eaters called sauropods. They had very long necks that could reach high into the trees, and a long tail to balance with. Small dinosaurs fed on insects, plants, and each other. Their **fossils** are not easily found as they were often eaten whole by bigger dinosaurs.

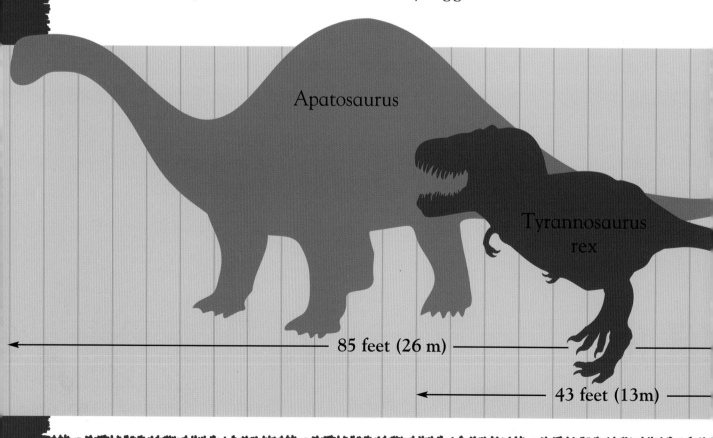

Apatosaurus

Tyrannosaurus rex

85 feet (26 m)

43 feet (13m)

Sauropods

Argentinosaurus	*131 feet (40 m)*	*Diplodocus*	*92 feet (28 m)*
Paralititan	*131 feet (40 m)*	*Brachiosaurus*	*85 feet (26 m)*
Ultrasaurus	*98 feet (30 m)*	*Apatosaurus*	*85 feet (26 m)*

Big carnivores

Gigantosaurus carolinii	*46 feet (14 m)*
Spinosaurus	*39-49 feet (12-15 m)*
Tyrannosaurus rex	*39-49 feet (12-15 m)*

Medium-sized dinosaurs

Triceratops	*30 feet (9 m)*	*Stegosaurus*	*26 feet (8 m)*
Ankylosaurus	*23-33 feet (7-10 m)*		

Smallest dinosaurs

Microraptor	*16 inches (40 cm)*	*Wannanosaurus*	*3 feet (1 m)*
Compsognathus	*24 inches (60 cm)*	*Sinovenator*	*3 feet (1 m)*

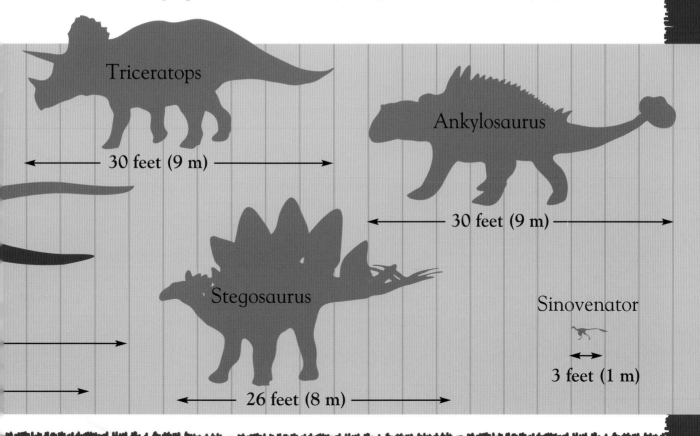

Triceratops — 30 feet (9 m)

Ankylosaurus — 30 feet (9 m)

Stegosaurus — 26 feet (8 m)

Sinovenator — 3 feet (1 m)

Predator or scavenger?

Was *Tyrannosaurus rex* a predator or a scavenger?
A predator is an animal that hunts other animals for food. A scavenger does not hunt. It feeds on animals that have already died or been killed by a predator.

Was it a predator?
Tyrannosaurus rex had forward-pointing eyes that gave it what scientists call **binocular** vision. Humans have binocular vision. Animals with this kind of vision are usually hunters. *Tyrannosaurus's* jaws were huge and filled with long notched teeth. Teeth like this could only belong to a predator. *Tyrannosaurus rex* must have been able to run fast in short bursts because it had very powerful leg muscles. A scavenger would not need to be able to do this.

forward-pointing but small eyes

long notched teeth

very small arms

strong but bulky legs

Was it a scavenger?

The eyes of a *Tyrannosaurus rex* were too small to be able to see prey in the distance. Its arms were too small to be able to hold on to anything it caught. Although its legs were big, they were bulky and good only for walking. Predators had to be able to run, so it must have been a scavenger.

The answer!

No one knows the right answer to this question. Most likely *Tyrannosaurus rex* was a predator that hunted for live meat but also scavenged for food too.

Glossary

ambush A surprise attack by something or someone who is hiding

ancient A very long time ago

binocular To make far away objects seem closer and larger

carnivore An animal that eats the flesh of other animals

crevice A narrow opening

cower To crouch in fear

erupt A violent explosion

fossil The hardened remains of an organism that lived thousands of years ago

organism Any living thing such as plants and animals

predator An animal that hunts other animals for food

prehistoric Before the time when events were recorded by humans

prey An animals that is hunted by another

reeds Tall, hollow-stemmed grasses that grow in swamps

scavenger An animal that feeds on dead animals

Index

Further Reading and Websites

Tyrannosaurus Rex by Elaine Landau. Children's Press, 2007.

Tyrannosaurus Rex by Joanne Mattern. Weekly Reader Early Learning Library, 2007.

Websites:

www.smithsonianeducation.org